Conford, Ellen.

What's cooking,
Jenny Archer?

$9.70

DATE			

4 WEEKS

What's Cooking, Jenny Archer?

What's Cooking, Jenny Archer?

by Ellen Conford

Illustrated by Diane Palmisciano

Little, Brown and Company

Boston   Toronto   London

Conford

Text copyright © 1989 by Conford Enterprises Ltd.
Illustrations copyright © 1989 by Diane Palmisciano

First Edition

Springboard Books and design is a trademark of Little, Brown
and Company (Inc.).

Library of Congress Cataloging-in-Publication Data

Conford, Ellen.
    What's cooking, Jenny Archer? / by Ellen Conford; illustrated
by Diane Palmisciano.
    p.   cm. (A Springboard book)
    Summary: Follows the comic mishaps of Jenny Archer as she
goes into business preparing lunches for friends at school.
    ISBN 0-316-15254-4
    [1. Cookery — Fiction.   2. Moneymaking projects — Fiction.
3. Schools — Fiction.   4. Humorous stories.]   I. Palmisciano,
Diane, ill.   II. Title.
PZ7.C7593Wg   1989
[Fic] — dc20   89-8251
                                                          CIP
                                                           AC

10 9 8 7 6 5 4 3 2 1

WOR

Published simultaneously in Canada
by Little, Brown & Company (Canada) Limited

PRINTED IN THE UNITED STATES OF AMERICA

This book — except for pages 8 to 9½ —
is for Johanna Hurwitz,
who is always an inspiration.
Pages 8 to 9½, however, are dedicated to U. H.

What's Cooking, Jenny Archer?

1

Jenny Archer was hungry.

She looked inside the refrigerator. Barkley, her big black dog, stood next to her. He was wagging his tail. The refrigerator was one of his favorite places.

"Don't hold the door open so long," her mother said. "Decide what you want to eat first."

"How can I decide what to eat if I can't see what we have?" asked Jenny.

"Why are you so hungry this afternoon? If you eat now you won't have any room for dinner."

"I'm not just hungry," said Jenny. "I'm *starving*. I'll have plenty of room for dinner."

She took out a jar of mint jelly, a loaf of raisin bread, and a package of bologna. She spread jelly on a piece of raisin bread. She put two slices of bologna on top of the jelly. She folded the bread over.

"That's a strange sandwich," her mother said.

"Why?" asked Jenny. "It's all stuff I like." She took a big bite and rubbed her stomach. "*Mmm.*"

"Didn't you eat lunch today?" her mother asked.

"I ate some of it," said Jenny. "But it was 'C' day."

"What's 'C' day?"

"Chow mein, cooked carrots, and cup custard. I ate the custard."

"Did you eat lunch yesterday?" asked Mrs. Archer.

"Yesterday was 'F' day. Fish sticks, french fries, and fruit salad," said Jenny. "I ate the french fries and the fruit salad."

She pulled the crust off her bread and gave it to Barkley. He wolfed it down.

"I think you'd better bring your own lunch from now on," her mother said.

"I think so, too," said Jenny.

"Let's see what we can use for lunches." Mrs. Archer opened the refrigerator and looked inside. Barkley looked in the refrigerator with Mrs. Archer.

Jenny noticed that her mother kept the door open as she looked. But she didn't say anything.

"We don't have very much in here," said Mrs. Archer. "Some leftover baked beans. A little dish of sliced beets. And some blue cheese." She laughed. "I could make you a 'B' lunch."

Jenny made a face. "*Ugh!*"

"I was only kidding," her mother said. "I didn't plan to go shopping before Saturday. But we'd better go now."

Jenny nodded. "By Saturday I would be very thin."

"Why don't you make a list?" said Mrs. Archer. "We can stock up for the rest of the week."

"Good idea." Jenny took a pencil and a piece of paper from the pad next to the telephone. She sat down at the table.

Deviled ham, she wrote. *Cheese. (Not blue cheese.)*

She tapped her pencil against her teeth. She pushed her glasses back on her nose.

Shrimp salad. Sweet pickles.

Now she was writing very fast. *Clam dip. Pita bread. Mushrooms.*

She reached the bottom of the page. She turned it over to start on the other side.

"That's a pretty long list," said Mrs. Archer.

"It's not so long," Jenny said. "This is just a small piece of paper."

"We'd better get moving," said Mrs. Archer. "It's getting pretty close to dinnertime."

"That's okay," said Jenny. "I'm not very hungry anyway."

2

After dinner that night, Jenny watched one of her favorite TV shows. It was called "Kids in the Kitchen." Danny and Denise were the two young chefs.

Every week the kids would prepare a special dish. Sometimes they baked a cake. Sometimes they cooked a whole meal.

"Today we'll show you how to make lunch-box lunches that will turn your friends lime green with envy."

"Perfect!" Jenny clapped. "Isn't this great, Barkley? Just what I need."

Barkley rested his head on his paws. He wasn't interested in food he couldn't smell.

"Use your imagination," said Danny. "Try new combinations."

Jenny nodded. "Like bologna, raisin bread, and mint jelly."

"Instead of plain old peanut butter and jelly, try a peanut butter, bacon, and banana sandwich."

Yum, Jenny thought.

"Cream cheese is a sandwich favorite," said Denise. "But you don't have to have it with jelly, either."

She chopped up walnuts and olives. She mixed them with some cream cheese.

She held up a jar. "This is chutney. It's from India. It's sweet and spicy and tastes great with cream cheese."

Sounds good, Jenny thought.

Denise shredded carrots and mixed them with raisins. She added them to another bowl of cream cheese.

Jenny watched, her eyes wide with amazement. She had no idea that there were so many creative things you could do with cream cheese.

"Food tastes better when it looks pretty," Denise said. She showed how to cut radishes so they looked like roses. Danny cut up celery stalks and shaped them into fans. He peeled carrots into thin strips with a vegetable peeler. He curled the strips around his finger. He used toothpicks to hold them in circles.

Jenny had never seen such elegant vegetables.

"Take a sandwich, a fruit, a vegetable, and maybe a small, sweet treat," said Denise, "and you'll have a delicious, well-balanced lunch."

When the show was over, Jenny ran downstairs to the kitchen. Her mother and father were drinking coffee. She opened the refrigerator door. Barkley trotted to her side.

"You can't be hungry," her mother said.

"I'm thinking about lunch," Jenny said.

"But we just ate dinner," said Mr. Archer.

"I'm thinking about tomorrow's lunch," Jenny said. "I watched 'Kids in the Kitchen.' I'm going to make all my own lunches."

"That's wonderful!" her mother said. "We're always so rushed in the morning."

"Do we have any chutney?" Jenny asked. "It's sweet and spicy and it's from India."

"No," her mother said.

"Maybe I'll start making another shopping list," Jenny said.

Mrs. Archer shook her head. "We're not shopping again until Saturday. You'll have to make your lunch without chutney."

"That's okay," said Jenny. "The Kids in the Kitchen gave me a lot of really good ideas. My friends are going to be lime green with envy when they see what I'm eating."

"Not if you're eating bologna and jelly sandwiches." Her mother laughed.

3

Jenny's parents left for work at eight-fifteen every morning. Jenny didn't have to go to school until eight-forty-five. She had plenty of time to prepare her lunch.

She made a deviled ham and sweet pickle sandwich on wheat bread. She put toothpicks in three cherry tomatoes. Then she stuck a green olive on top of each little tomato. She put them in a plastic sandwich bag.

She cut a wedge of honeydew melon into pieces. She stuck a toothpick into each piece.

"I'd better put toothpicks on the shopping list," she told herself. Creative cooking seemed to use a lot of toothpicks.

She took two oatmeal cookies from a small package. She was sure her friends would be lime green with envy when they saw her lunch.

She took two more oatmeal cookies so she could share them.

She put everything in her old King Kong lunch box.

Sandwich, vegetable, fruit, dessert. A very balanced lunch.

Jenny was surprised. She hadn't known cooking could be this easy.

At eight-forty-five she met her friends Wilson Wynn and Beth Moore. They waited for her at the corner of Lemon Street every morning.

"Neat lunch box," said Wilson. "Aren't you eating the school lunch today?"

"I'm never going to eat the school lunch again," Jenny said. "I'm making my own from now on."

"Lucky you," said Beth.

"I wish my mother would make me lunch," Wilson said. "But she never has time. Tyler is always cranky in the morning." Tyler was Wilson's baby brother.

"Why don't you make your own lunch?" Jenny said.

"Me?" said Wilson. "I can't cook."

"It's not very hard," said Jenny.

"What did you bring today?" Beth asked. Jenny told her.

"That sounds good," said Wilson.

"It sure does," Beth said.

"Stop!" said Wilson suddenly. He turned to Jenny and held up his hand like a crossing guard. "I have a great idea!" I'll give you

my lunch money if you'll make my lunch every day."

Jenny did some arithmetic in her head. The school lunch cost $1.50. $1.50 times 5 days a week = $7.50 a week.

Seven dollars and fifty cents a week! Just for making one extra lunch!

"Wilson, you're a genius!" said Beth.

"Thank you," he said.

"Will you make my lunch too, Jenny?" she begged. "Please!"

Jenny pushed her glasses back on her nose. She did some more arithmetic in her head. $7.50 a week times 2 people = $15.

Fifteen dollars a week just to make two extra lunches! It sounded like a lot of money for very little work.

"You really could do it yourselves," said Jenny. "All you need is a little imagination."

"You have enough imagination for all of us," said Wilson.

Jenny shook her head. "I don't know if it's right for you to pay me."

"But *we* asked you to make our lunches," said Beth. "We *want* to pay you."

"Well . . ." said Jenny. "Okay. It's a deal."

"Yay!" shouted Beth.

"Double yay!" said Wilson.

I'm going to be rich, thought Jenny.

4

At lunchtime Jenny and Beth sat down together. They put their trays on the table. Jenny's tray was empty. But Beth had the school lunch. Chicken noodle soup, pizza, canned peas, and a slice of peach pie.

"That's not a very well balanced lunch," said Jenny. She reached into her lunch box.

Beth watched as Jenny unwrapped her sandwich. She spread the rest of her lunch on the tray.

"Everything looks so good," Beth said. She sounded very hungry.

Jenny handed her a toothpick with a cherry tomato and an olive on it.

Beth popped it into her mouth. "Yum. And I don't even like olives."

Now the other kids at the table were watching Jenny eat.

April Adams had brought her lunch from home. "Tuna fish and a Twinkie," she said. "I'm so tired of tuna fish and Twinkies."

Jenny passed around melon pieces. There were six kids at the table. She had only seven chunks of melon. But her friends looked so lime green with envy that she had to share.

She gave away three of her oatmeal cookies. Beth said the pizza was so horrible she couldn't eat it. Jenny gave Beth half her sandwich.

Clifford Stern looked down at his chicken soup. "There's only one noodle in here!" he complained. "They should call this chicken-and-*one*-noodle soup."

"Jenny could make your lunches," Beth said suddenly. "She's going to make mine. And she charges the same as the school lunch. You'll just have to bring an extra dime for milk."

"Wait a minute!" Jenny said. "I'm not sure I can —"

"Would you?" Clifford asked.

"Would you make mine too?" asked April.

"I don't know," said Jenny. "I'd have to make four extra lunches every day." She thought for a moment. "I could get up a little earlier."

She pushed her glasses back on her nose. She took a pencil from her pocket. She wrote some numbers on her napkin.

$1.50 times 5 days = $7.50.

$7.50 times 4 people = $30.00.

Thirty dollars a week! Just for making four extra lunches!

"It's a deal," she said.

"Great!" said Clifford.

"You're saving my life," said April.

I wonder, thought Jenny, how much a motorcycle costs?

5

When her mother got home that afternoon, Jenny was standing in front of the refrigerator. Barkley was next to her, wagging his tail.

"Are you hungry again?" asked Mrs. Archer.

"I'm starving," said Jenny.

"But you took your own lunch today."

"My lunch was so good I had to share it with everybody. I hardly ate a thing."

Mrs. Archer laughed. "Maybe you should

make extra-big lunches so you'll have enough for everybody."

"That's just what I was thinking," said Jenny. "Sort of."

She was about to tell her mother about her new business when Mrs. Archer yawned. "I'm so tired," she said. "I'd like to lie down for a while."

"Okay," said Jenny. "I'll plan tomorrow's lunch."

"Plan first," said Mrs. Archer, "with the door closed."

Jenny closed the refrigerator door. Mrs. Archer went upstairs. Jenny heard the bed squeak as her mother lay down.

She opened the refrigerator door again. She looked for something good to snack on.

The next morning Jenny was already in the kitchen when her father and mother came downstairs.

"Hi, early bird." Jenny's father ruffled her hair.

"What do you think of a clam dip and mushroom sandwich?" she asked.

"For breakfast?" Mr. Archer sounded startled.

"Of course not," said Jenny. "For lunch."

"It sounds a bit strange to me," said her father.

"A good cook needs a little imagination," Jenny said.

Mrs. Archer laughed. "If you need a little imagination to be a good cook, you're going to be a *great* cook."

"Thank you," said Jenny. "I think I will too."

Jenny wanted to tell them about her new lunch business. But they were hurrying to get ready for work. She would tell them when they got home.

As soon as they left, Jenny washed her hands carefully. The Kids in the Kitchen always said, "The first rule of good cooking is clean hands."

She had deviled ham for two deviled ham and sweet pickle sandwiches. She made two clam dip and mushroom sandwiches. She made one shrimp salad sandwich.

She took five stalks of celery. She cut the white ends into fans. Jenny's celery fans weren't like the ones Dennis had made. Hers looked more like brooms.

But they were much fancier than plain, old celery. She tried to make radish roses. But she couldn't remember how to cut them.

It didn't really matter. Jenny hated radishes.

She cut little squares of cheddar cheese. She put toothpicks in each square. She was definitely going to need a new box of toothpicks very soon.

She cut five thin pieces from the carrot cake. The cake was left over from last night's dessert.

In half an hour she made five delicious, healthy lunches. She could feel the six dollars in her pocket already.

Beth and Wilson were waiting for her at the corner of Lemon Street. Jenny carried five brown paper bags. Three in her right hand, two in her left hand.

"What did you make us?" Wilson asked.

"Wait till you see," said Jenny. "You'll love it." She held out one of the bags. Wilson gave her a dollar bill and two quarters.

Wilson opened the bag and looked inside. "It smells funny," he said. "It smells like . . . the beach."

"That's because it's clams," said Jenny.

"I don't like clams." Wilson took his money out of Jenny's hand.

"It's not just plain clams," Jenny said. "It's clam dip."

"I don't like clam dip," said Wilson. He put his money back in his pocket.

"I can't eat clams," said Beth. "I'm allergic to them."

"Can you eat shrimp salad?" asked Jenny.

Beth shook her head. "I'm allergic to shrimp, too."

Jenny began to worry. What if Clifford and April couldn't eat clams or shrimp either?

"I like shrimp," Wilson said.

"Okay," Jenny said. "You can have the shrimp salad lunch."

"Yay!" Wilson pulled his money out of his pocket and gave it back to Jenny.

"Do you want a deviled ham and sweet pickle sandwich?" she asked Beth.

"Like you had yesterday?" said Beth. "Sure. That was good."

"Okay." Jenny handed her a bag.

Someone will like clam dip and mushrooms, Jenny told herself. Wilson is just too young for such a classy sandwich.

*   *   *

At lunchtime Jenny gave Clifford Stern and April Adams their choice of sandwiches.

"Deviled ham!" Clifford said. He grabbed the bag that Jenny held out.

"All I ever get is tuna fish and peanut butter," said April. "I'll try the clam and mushroom sandwich."

"You have grown-up taste," Jenny said. "Like me."

Beth and April thought the little squares of cheese were cute. Clifford said the celery broom was neat. April picked all the mushrooms out of her sandwich.

But she loved the carrot cake. "Much better than a Twinkie," she said.

At the end of the lunch period, Sarah Faith and Howard Berry asked Jenny if she would make lunch for them, too.

Jenny felt the four dollar bills and eight quarters in her pocket. If she made lunch for Sarah and Howard she would earn three more dollars a day. She would have nine dollars a day!

She started scribbling on her napkin.

$9 a day times 5 days a week = $45.00.

Forty-five dollars a week! Just for making six extra lunches!

"It's a deal," she said.

"Thank you," said Sarah.

"Thank you," said Howard.

I think I'll get my own American Express card, Jenny decided.

6

On the way home Jenny stopped at Mr. Marvel's Deli. She knew she didn't have enough food at home for six extra lunches. She remembered that Wilson didn't like clams. And April had picked the mushrooms out of her sandwich. And Beth was allergic.

I'll get something everybody likes, she thought.

"Hi, Jenny," said Mr. Marvel. "What can I do for you?"

Jenny looked around the store. Mr. Marvel had glass cases full of all kinds of meats, homemade salads, and cheeses. He even had dishes of rice pudding and Jell-O.

"I need meat for seven sandwiches," Jenny said. "Everybody likes roast beef, don't they?"

Mr. Marvel nodded. "Roast beef is very popular."

"Okay. I want three slices for each sandwich," Jenny said. "How much is that?"

"It's about a pound and a half," said Mr. Marvel. "That will cost about nine dollars."

"*Nine dollars?*" Jenny gasped. "I never knew roast beef was that expensive."

"You can get sliced chicken for seven sandwiches for six-fifty," Mr. Marvel said.

Jenny took the four dollar bills and eight quarters out of her pocket. There was still some clam dip left at home. She could make another clam dip and mushroom sandwich for herself.

Wilson liked shrimp salad. There was just enough left for one sandwich. She was sure the other kids would like chicken. Everybody liked chicken. She would need only enough for five sandwiches.

"I'll take fifteen slices of chicken."

Mr. Marvel wrapped the chicken in white paper. He put it in a brown bag. "That's five-fifty."

But what about dessert? All the carrot cake was gone. She had eaten the last three oatmeal cookies for a snack. She was sure her customers would want dessert with their lunch.

"Do you have any cookies for fifty cents?" she asked.

Mr. Marvel showed her a large, plastic-wrapped cookie.

"This is fifty cents."

"Fifty cents for *one cookie?*" She couldn't believe it.

"It's a very big cookie," said Mr. Marvel.

"Not big enough for seven people." She gave Mr. Marvel five dollars and fifty cents. All she had left was two quarters.

Looking at all that food had made her hungry.

"I'll take the cookie, too," she said.

Jenny munched on her cookie as she walked home. She had earned six dollars today. But she had to pay five-fifty for chicken. And that was just for sandwiches for one day. It didn't even include fruit or dessert.

What would she make for lunch after tomorrow?

Jenny had a terrible thought. What if she had to pay more for food than she got paid for the lunches? She might *lose* money if she had too many customers!

She remembered what the Kids in the Kitchen said. "All you need is a little imagination."

Jenny had lots of imagination. She would find a way to make creative lunches and get rich at the same time.

Or at least she would find a way to make creative lunches and not get poor.

7

Barkley ran to meet Jenny when she came home. She always took him for a walk right after school. But today Barkley seemed more interested in the bag from Marvel's Deli.

He sniffed and sniffed at it. He could smell the chicken inside.

"No, Barkley," she said sternly. "Don't even think about it."

She put the bag in the refrigerator.

She clipped Barkley's leash to his collar and

took him outside. As they walked, she tried to think of a way to save money on food.

When they got back to the house, Jenny knew what she had to do.

She washed her hands.

"It's always cheaper to make your own food than to buy it," she told Barkley. Barkley wagged his tail. He understood the word "food."

"Fifty cents for one cookie!" she said.

Barkley wagged his tail harder. He understood the word "cookie," too.

"I'm going to bake my own cookies," Jenny said. "That will save me a lot of money."

She had never made cookies before. But the Kids in the Kitchen had. It looked pretty easy.

She found a package of chocolate bits in the cabinet over the stove. Mrs. Archer didn't bake much. But they all liked snacking on chocolate chips.

There was a recipe for chocolate chip cookies right on the package. The recipe made thirty cookies. That would be enough until Friday.

Jenny began to gather the things she would need. Flour. Salt. Eggs. Butter or margarine. Baking powder.

Baking powder.

Jenny looked into every cabinet in the kitchen. She couldn't find any baking powder.

But the recipe only called for a teaspoon and a half of baking powder. That was such a little bit. Nobody would know if she left it out.

She couldn't find any brown sugar either. But there was plenty of white sugar. "It doesn't matter," she told Barkley. "Sugar is sugar."

Jenny turned the oven on.

She put everything in a big bowl and began to mix it. The batter was very thick. It was hard to stir. Jenny added a little milk. That worked fine. Now the batter was much easier to mix.

Jenny used a teaspoon to drop small circles of batter onto a baking sheet. The batter spread out a lot. Jenny thought they would be nice, big cookies.

She put the cookie sheet into the oven. She set the oven timer for ten minutes.

"No wonder cookies are so expensive," she said to Barkley. "Making cookies is very hard work."

She went upstairs to feed Phyllis, her gold-fish. Just as she tapped the food into the fish-bowl, the phone rang.

It was Clifford Stern. Jenny was surprised. Clifford had never called her before.

"What are you making for lunch tomor-row?" he asked.

"Chicken sandwiches."

"I don't like chicken," said Clifford.

"Everybody likes chicken!" Jenny said.

"Not me."

"I'll make you something else then," she said. "I'm a very creative cook."

"The school lunch is hot dogs tomorrow," Clifford said. "I like hot dogs."

"But I'm making chocolate chip cookies," Jenny said. "Plus a surprise." She didn't know what the surprise would be yet. But she was sure she could think of one.

"What kind of surprise?" Clifford asked.

"If I told you it wouldn't be a surprise."

"Well, okay," said Clifford. "But it better be good."

"Don't worry," Jenny said. "It will be —"

Something smelled. Jenny sniffed. What was it? Smoke?

"YIKES!" Jenny dropped the phone and ran downstairs. She grabbed two potholders. She opened the oven door.

Black smoke poured out.

"My cookies!" she cried. "They're all burnt!"

She looked at the black mess on the cookie sheet. The cookies had only been in the oven for eight minutes.

44

The recipe must be wrong, she thought. Bake at 475° for ten minutes. She checked the recipe again. Bake at 375° for ten minutes.

Jenny wanted to cry. She turned the oven off. The kitchen was filled with smoke.

She opened the back door and waved a dishtowel at the smoke. The air began to clear.

She saw that she still had half the cookie batter left. She could try again.

The front door opened.

Jenny heard her mother's voice. "Hi, Jenny . . . Jenny? WHAT'S BURNING?"

8

Mrs. Archer ran into the kitchen.

"Nothing's burning now," said Jenny. "But my cookies are ruined."

Mrs. Archer looked around. There were floury footprints and pawprints all over the floor. There were eggshells on the table. There were spoons and cups and sugar and margarine all over the place. Jenny had dropped bits of batter on a chair.

Mrs. Archer put her hand over her eyes. "This is the worst mess I've ever seen."

"Don't worry," said Jenny. "I'll clean it all up."

"You certainly will," said her mother. "And I don't want you to use the stove when I'm not home."

"I didn't know I wasn't supposed to," Jenny said. "You never told me that."

"That's because you never used it before."

"Can I put in the rest of the cookies?" Jenny said.

"I guess so," said her mother. "But be careful. And *clean this kitchen!*"

Jenny scraped the burnt cookies off the cookie sheet. She greased it again. She dropped the cookie batter onto it.

This time Jenny set the oven temperature to 375°. She set the timer for ten minutes. She began to clean up as the cookies baked. Now the smell coming from the oven was wonderful.

When the timer buzzed, Jenny opened the oven door.

The cookies smelled fine. But they looked strange. The drops had all run together into a thin cookie that spread over the whole baking sheet. It wasn't dark, like chocolate chip cookies are. It was very pale and very flat.

"This doesn't look like cookies, Barkley," Jenny said. Barkley wagged his tail. He didn't care how cookies looked. He just wanted some.

Jenny looked unhappily at her cookie. She looked at the mess she still had to clean up. She wondered what surprise she could bring Clifford tomorrow.

How come, Jenny wondered, this never happened to the Kids in the Kitchen?

9

The next morning Mrs. Archer saw the package of chicken that Jenny had bought at Marvel's Deli.

"Where did this come from?" she asked.

"I bought it," Jenny said. "I needed it for my lunches."

"How many lunches do you eat a day?" her father asked.

"I only eat one. The rest are for my customers."

"Customers?" her mother repeated.

"Uh oh," said Mr. Archer.

Jenny told her parents all about her new business.

"That's why I baked the cookies. I mean, the cookie. I make nine dollars a day! And this is just the beginning."

"I'm not sure this is a good idea," Mrs. Archer said.

"It's a great idea," Jenny said. "Or it will be. Once I earn more money on the lunches than I spend on the food."

Barkley wagged his tail.

"Jenny, there are laws about preparing food for other people," her father said. "Restaurants have to get special licenses."

"But I'm not a restaurant," said Jenny.

"What if someone gets sick after eating your lunch?" her mother asked.

"My lunches are very healthy!" Jenny said. "No one will get sick from them."

"There are other problems to think about,"

her father said. "But there's no time now. We'll talk tonight."

"Okay," said Jenny. "But I have to bring the lunches today. I promised."

After her parents left, Jenny washed her hands. She unwrapped the chicken. She put seven slices of bread on the table. She placed three slices of chicken on five pieces of bread. She spooned shrimp salad onto one piece for Wilson.

The doorbell rang. Who could that be so early in the morning?

She ran to the door. "Who is it?" she called.

"It's me," said Wilson. "Wilson."

Jenny opened the door.

"I came to get my lunch. My mother is taking me to the dentist this morning. I can't walk to school with you. So I need my lunch now."

"I'm making it right now," said Jenny. "Come on in."

Wilson stepped inside. He looked around. "Where's Barkley?" he whispered. Wilson didn't like dogs.

Where *was* Barkley? Jenny wondered. He always ran to the door when the bell rang.

"I guess he's still in the kitchen," said Jenny.

In the kitchen!

"Oh, no!" she cried.

She ran into the kitchen. Barkley raced past her and crawled behind the couch.

Jenny looked at the table. All the chicken was gone. The white wrapping was on the floor. Three slices of bread were missing.

"Oh, Barkley," she cried. "How could you do this to me?" She clapped her hand to her forehead. "What am I going to do now?"

10

"Did Barkley eat my lunch?" Wilson asked.

"He ate *everybody's* lunch," said Jenny. "And I don't have money to buy any more food."

"I have my dollar fifty for lunch," Wilson said. "You could borrow it."

"Thanks, Wilson," Jenny said sadly. "But a dollar fifty isn't enough to make six extra lunches."

"I guess I'd better buy the school lunch today," he said.

"I guess so."

Wilson left. Jenny told Barkley what a bad dog he was. He tapped his tail lightly on the floor. He laid his head down on his paws. He knew he was a bad dog.

Jenny went back into the kitchen. She looked around. There was still plenty of bread. She just didn't have anything to put between the slices.

The giant cookie was on the counter next to the oven. She could break it into cookie-sized pieces.

She looked at the clock. She had to leave for school in fifteen minutes.

She thought about all her customers. She thought how unhappy they'd be if she didn't bring their lunches. She thought about the nine dollars she wasn't going to make.

I'm not going to give up, Jenny told herself. Just because I have one or two little problems. There must be plenty of stuff for sandwiches here.

She washed her hands again.

She opened a jar of peanut butter. She took a package of cream cheese and a cucumber from the refrigerator.

The Kids in the Kitchen had mixed cream cheese and peanut butter with all kinds of interesting things. It just takes a little imagination, she thought.

She worked as fast as she could. She had the new sandwiches made in fifteen minutes.

But she had no paper bags. There were only small plastic bags for the sandwiches and cookie pieces. How could she get six extra lunches to school without lunch bags?

Aha! Jenny thought. I'm a genius. She reached under the sink for a large lawn-and-leaf bag. But there weren't any. They were out of *everything* in this house!

The doorbell rang again. "Where are you?" called Beth. "We're going to be late!"

"Wait a minute," Jenny said. "I just had another great idea!"

11

Everyone stared at Jenny when she walked into her classroom that morning. She was carrying a large, blue suitcase.

"Why did you bring the suitcase, Jenny?" asked Mrs. Pike.

"To carry lunch in," Jenny said.

"You must eat a very big lunch!" Mrs. Pike said. All the kids laughed. "Put it in the back for now."

At twelve o'clock Jenny carried the suitcase to the lunchroom. The kids gathered around her eagerly. She handed Clifford, April, Howard, and Sarah their plastic bags.

They each gave her $1.50. Jenny put the money in her pocket. She rubbed the dollar bills together. The quarters jingled. They made a wonderful sound. And her pocket felt nice and heavy.

Clifford unwrapped his sandwich. He took a bite.

"Hey! What is this? This is a weird sandwich."

Jenny looked. "You've got a cream cheese, pineapple, and cucumber sandwich."

"You said we were having chicken!"

"But you don't like chicken," Jenny said. "I thought you wanted something different."

"This is too different," Clifford said. "And where's the surprise?"

April took a bite of her sandwich. "This is

peanut butter. Jenny, remember, I told you I was sick of peanut butter."

"But it's not just plain peanut butter," Jenny said. "There are apples and raisins mixed in. It's a very creative sandwich."

"I want my money back," said Clifford.

Jenny looked at Howard. He was making a terrible face. "Me too," he said. "Cream cheese isn't supposed to be crunchy."

"I put walnuts in it," Jenny said.

"And it's *green*."

"Those are the olives. Really, Howard, it's a very grown-up type of sandwich."

"Maybe I'll like it when I'm grown up," Howard said. "But now I want my money back."

"What's this?" Sarah held up a piece of Jenny's cookie.

"That's a chocolate chip cookie," Jenny said.

Sarah took a bite. "No, it's not. I never

tasted a chocolate chip cookie like this. I want my money back."

Clifford pushed his sandwich across the table. "I want my money back, too."

"So do I," said Howard.

"It cost me a lot of money to make those lunches," Jenny said.

"They don't taste like it," said Howard.

"This isn't fair," Jenny said. "We had a deal. You can't back out now."

"I want my money back, I want my money back!" Clifford chanted.

Sarah and Howard joined in. "We want our money back! We want our money back!"

Mrs. Riley, the lunchroom aide, hurried to the table. "What's going on? Why are you shouting?"

"She took our lunch money," Sarah said. "And she won't give it back."

"That's not true!" said Jenny.

"Do you have their money?" Mrs. Riley asked her.

"Yes, but —"

"Give it back," said Mrs. Riley.

"But they said —"

Mrs. Riley wouldn't listen. *"Give them back their money."*

Jenny sighed. She reached into her pocket. She pulled out three dollar bills and six quarters. "This is *really* not fair," she said. Mrs. Riley just frowned.

Sarah, Clifford, and Howard grabbed their money. They went to wait on the lunch line. Mrs. Riley gave Jenny one last frown and walked away.

"Don't you want your money back, too, April?" asked Jenny.

"No," said April. "A deal's a deal. But I think I'll make my own lunches from now on."

Jenny turned to Beth. "At least you like my cooking," she said.

Beth didn't answer. She just kept eating her

sandwich. It was peanut butter and cranberry sauce.

"You don't really like it, do you?" asked Jenny.

"It's good," said Beth. "Really."

Jenny had a feeling that Beth's fingers were crossed behind her back.

"You're a true friend," Jenny told her. "But I think I just went out of the lunch business."

12

When Mrs. Archer came home from work that afternoon, Jenny was looking inside the refrigerator.

"Don't tell me you're hungry again!"

"I'm not," Jenny said. "I'm full. I ate one-and-a-half extra sandwiches today. I'm putting some leftover stuff back."

"Why did you eat so much?"

Jenny told her mother what had happened with Barkley and the chicken that morning.

Barkley crawled under the table and hid until Jenny stopped talking about him.

She told her mother about the sandwiches she made instead of chicken.

She told her that no one liked her creative lunches. She told her about Mrs. Riley and how unfair she was.

"It cost me five dollars and fifty cents to make those sandwiches," she said. "Even though they didn't have any chicken in them. I went to all that trouble and I only made three dollars."

"That's too bad," said Mrs. Archer.

Jenny nodded. "I thought I'd better stop before I lose any more money."

Mrs. Archer put her arm around Jenny. "You must be pretty disappointed," she said.

"Well, I was," Jenny said. "But I had a feeling you and Dad might make me stop anyway. And on the way home I had a great idea."

"Another great idea?" Mrs. Archer looked a little worried.

"Maybe *certain people* don't like my lunches," she said. "But I'm still a very creative cook."

"You sure are," said her mother.

"I might even be *too* creative to make lunches for school kids."

"That's probably true," her mother agreed.

"But soon I'm going to be a famous cook. Everyone will know my name."

"Why?" her mother asked.

"Because," said Jenny, "it's going to be on the front cover of the *Jenny Archer Cookbook!*"